I Know What You Do When I Go to School

Ann Edwards Cannon
Illustrated by Jennifer Mazzucco

GIBBS·SMITH
P
PUBLISHER

SALT LAKE CITY

04 03 02 01 5 4 3 2 1

Text Copyright © 1996 by Ann Edwards Cannon
Illustrations copyright © 1996 by Jennifer Mazzucco

Gibbs Smith, Publisher
P.O. Box 667
Layton, Utah 84041

Hand lettering by Jennifer Mazzucco

Printed and bound in China

Library of Congress Cataloging-in-Publication Data

Cannon. A. E. (Ann Edwards)
    I know what you do when I go to school/ Ann Cannon;
Illustrated by Jennifer Mazzucco.-- 1st ed.
        p. cm.
    "A Peregrine Smith book"-- T. p. verso.
    Summary: A child imagines all of the great adventures that his
mother and younger brother have while he is at school.
    ISBN 0-87905-743-2
    ISBN 1-58685-107-1 (pbk.)
    [1. Schools-- Fiction. 2. Imagination-- Fiction. 3. Mothers and
sons--Fiction.] I. Mazzucco, Jennifer, 1972-- ill. II. Title
P27.C171351af 1996
[Fic]--dc20
                        96-5219
                        CIP
                        AC

To Philip, who gave me the idea
A.E.C.

To my loving family- mom, dad, sue-
supportive friends- n.l. j.f. e.t. b.h.
& d.a. a.g. f.w. j.h.
J.M.

Hurry up, Howie!
You'll be late. Howie?

Mom, I've been thinking.
I know what you and
Wally do when I
go to school.

While I'm sitting at my desk pasting stars on paper, you get Wally dressed. He wants to wear his Batman pajama top. You say yes.

While I'm writing my name at the blackboard, you and Wally get out the soap bubbles and blow bubbles in every single room of the whole house. Even the living room.

Then you jump on
all the beds with
your shoes _on_.
But not until
you slide down
the bannister in
the hall. Wally
gets to go first.

While I'm counting out marbles from the marble jar for math, you and Wally dive through the laundry chute headfirst. You yell, "Geronimo!" Wally screams, "Cowabunga!"

After that, you use all the towels and sheets and blankets to make a humongous fort. Then you and Wally hide from the bad guys.

While I'm singing
"Itsy-bitsy Spider,"
you and Wally call
up people on the
telephone. You call
Dad...
and Grandma...
and Aunt Sandra.
Wally calls the
Easter Bunny.

While I'm feeding milkweed to the monarch caterpillars, you and Wally dig for dinosaur bones in the backyard. Fritz helps.

While I'm having a snack of crackers and fruit, you go to the grocery store and buy candy. Big bagfuls. More candy than even a starving giant could eat. It takes five shopping carts just to carry it out to the car. On your way home, you stop at the video store and rent movies. Wally gets to choose. He picks fifteen ninja movies, and _you_ don't even say no.

While I'm learning how to
tie my shoes, you go home
to watch the fifteen movies.
But first you pop popcorn.
Wally puts too much popcorn
in the popper, so the whole
entire kitchen fills up with
popcorn all the way to the
ceiling, and <u>you</u> don't even
yell. You and Wally just
climb out of a window
and onto the roof.

While I'm doing the crab walk across the gym floor for exercise, a helicopter lands on top of our house. You and Wally get inside and put on helmets. The pilot gives Wally his walkie-talkie. He lets you drive. Then you fly to a restaurant where you order pizza for lunch. My favorite.

Mom, I've been really thinking. I don't want to go to school.

Come here, Howie. Do you know what we do after lunch? Wally and I send that helicopter away, and we walk fifty-five miles all the way home, where we put up the bubbles and the blankets and the shovels we used to dig for dinosaur bones.

Then we make the beds
and rewind the videos and
throw away candy wrappers
and sweep up every last
piece of popcorn in the whole
entire house! You can bet
all this hard work makes
Wally tired, all right.
So can you guess what
I do next?

What?
I make Wally take
a great big boring,
long and fat
all - afternoon nap.
A nap?! Hmm.

Hey, Mom, I'm ready to go! Will you and Wally take me to school – please?